Duets for (

for **Flute**
with CD play-along

FILM

Arranged by
Barrie Carson Turner

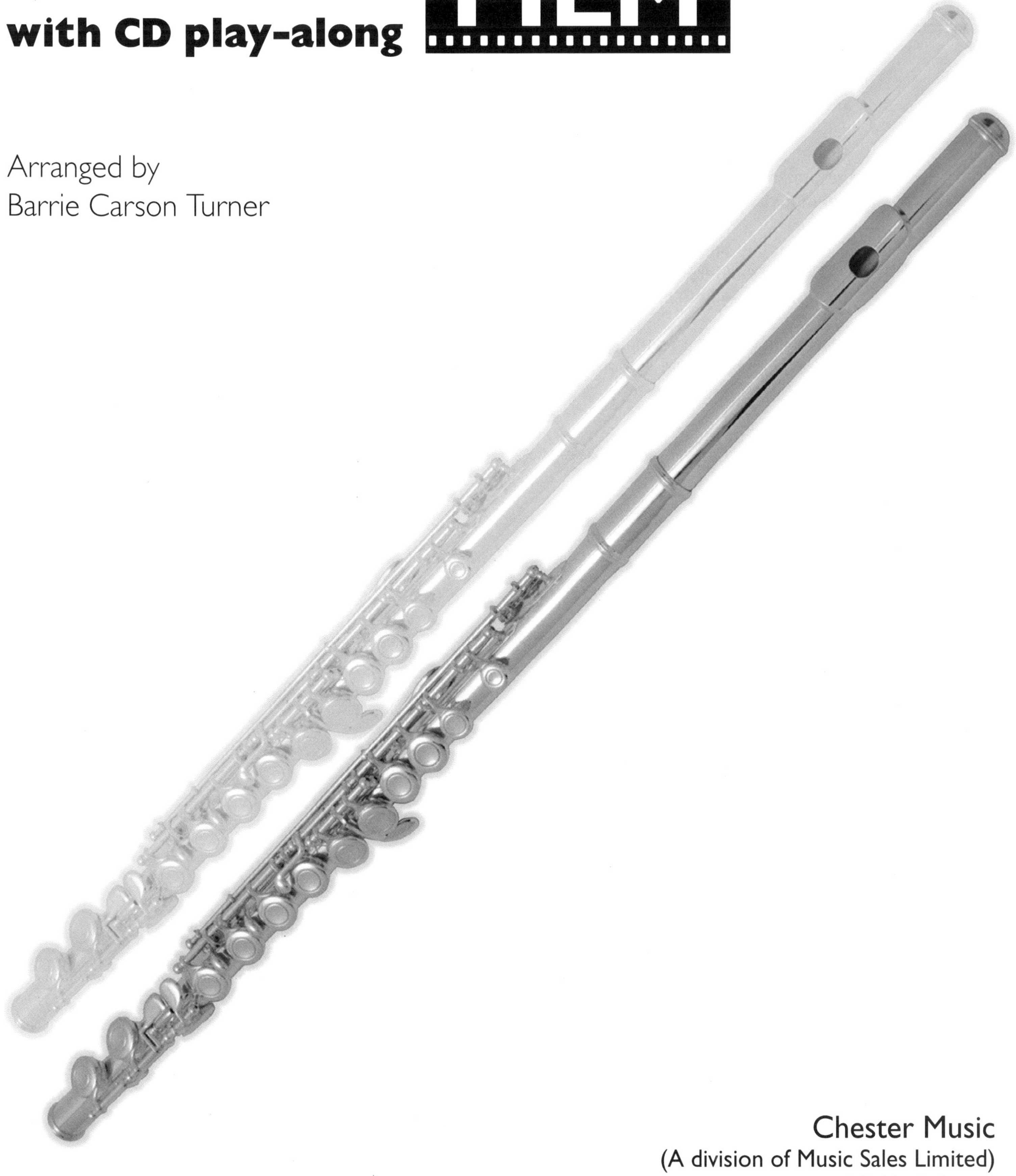

Chester Music
(A division of Music Sales Limited)
8/9 Frith Street
London W1D 3JB

INTRODUCTION

The early stages of learning an instrument can at times be frustrating and lonely - requiring lots of practice without being able to join an ensemble and enjoy playing with other musicians.

We put this book together to give flautists at the earliest stages the opportunity to have more fun - playing duets with great backing tracks whilst gaining all the benefits of ensemble playing.

All the tunes are popular and many you will know already. Listen to the complete performances on the CD with both flutes (tracks 2 - 15) to learn each piece; you may find it helps to practise by playing along with these parts.

Then you can select a part to play on your own with the CD by moving on to tracks 16 - 43. Once you have learnt one part, then you can move on to the other! The pieces in this book range from Grade 1 up to Grade 2+.

Alternatively, you can simply play these easy duets with a friend. However you decide to use this book, we hope you will have lots of fun whilst improving your flute playing.

Order No. CH61836 ISBN 0-7119-8596-0

Music processed by Enigma Music Production Services
Cover design by Ian Butterworth
Printed in Great Britain

CONTENTS

Waltz from "The Sleeping Beauty"
(*from* "Rollerball")

This ballet established Tchaikovsky as a leading ballet composer. Play the melody as smoothly as you can, and take care with the syncopation.

By Peter Ilyich Tchaikovsky

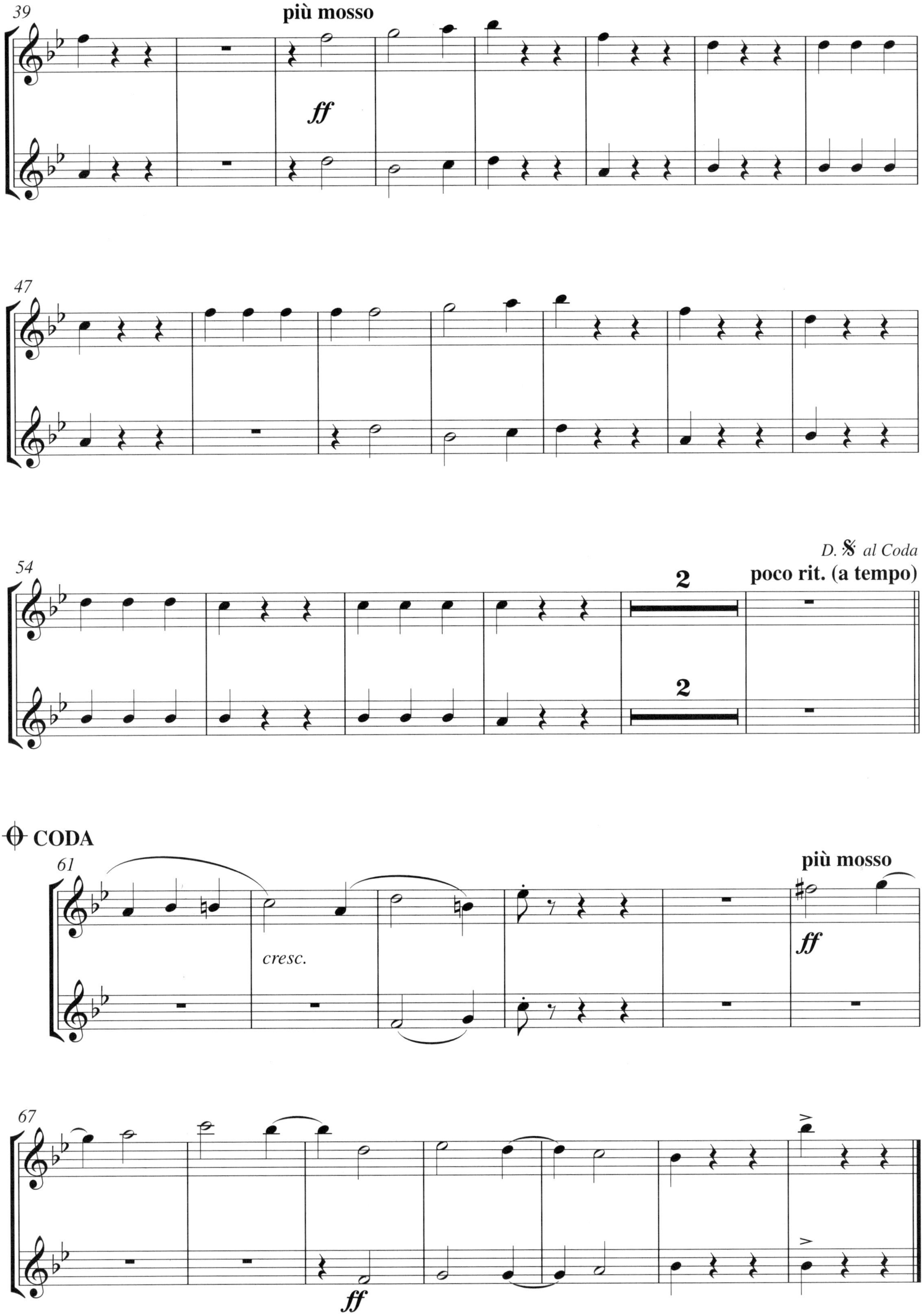
39
più mosso
ff
47
54
D. 𝄋 al Coda
poco rit. (a tempo)
2
2
CODA
61
cresc.
più mosso
ff
67
ff

Supercalifragilisticexpialidocious
(*from Walt Disney's* "Mary Poppins")

Play the melody of this piece in a light bouncy style, slightly accenting each minim.
In the harmony part, the minims should be staccato throughout.

Words & Music by Richard M. Sherman & Robert B. Sherman

Jean de Florette (Theme)

The melody and harmony parts of this piece have been arranged in question and answer style. The harmony part should flow imperceptibly out of the melody.

By Jean-Claude Petit

The Blue Danube

(*from* "2001: A Space Odyssey")

Composed in 1867, this is Johann Strauss's most well known waltz, and probably the most famous waltz of all time. It made its composer world famous overnight.

By Johann Strauss

Allegro (tempo di valse)

29
Fine
f
36
p
40
f
f
p
45
f
f
50
1.
2.
D. 𝄋 al Fine
p

The Bare Necessities
(*from Walt Disney's* "The Jungle Book")

Play this piece with a bright bounce, and in a light staccato style. If you are familiar with the words, say them to yourself as you play, to help you with the syncopated rhythms.

Words & Music by Terry Gilkyson

Moon River
(*from* "Breakfast at Tiffany's")

Give this beautiful melody your best legato playing. Notice the accent on the minim at the beginning of bar 32. This is the high point of the piece.

Words by Johnny Mercer
Music by Henry Mancini

Can't Take My Eyes Off You
(*from* "Bridget Jones' Diary")

Count the beginning of the melody part like this - 1,2,3 *and 4 and*, playing on 'and 4 and'.
In the harmony part, take care with the syncopated rhythm of the repeated notes.

Words & Music by Bob Crewe & Bob Gaudio

Fine
rall. (2nd time only)
(2nd time only)
18
f
f
22
26
30
dim.
33
D. 𝄋 al Fine
mp
mf

When You Say Nothing At All
(*from* "Notting Hill")

This song was sung by Ronan Keating in 1999.
Count carefully to ensure both parts start together. Don't miss the change of time in bar16.

Words & Music by Don Schlitz & Paul Overstreet

Not too fast

19
22
25
dim.
29
mp
32
rall.

Scene from "Swan Lake"
(*from* "Billy Elliot")

Tchaikovsky's ballet *Swan Lake* was first performed in Moscow in 1877. At its first performance, the ballet was a terrible failure; but today it is one of the composer's best loved works.

By Peter Ilyich Tchaikovsky

Hallelujah Chorus (from "The Messiah")
(*from* "Look Who's Talking Too")

At the first London performance of this piece, the King and audience were so captivated by the music, that they stood up. This tradition of standing for the music continues today.

By George Frideric Handel

Just The Two Of Us
(*from* "Austin Powers 2")

Notice that the harmony part begins this piece, which is rhythmically quite difficult. Play the music slowly, counting eight quavers per bar, until you become familiar with the music.

Words & Music by Ralph MacDonald, William Salter & Bill Withers

Moderately

19
f
23
27
30
33

Raiders' March
(*from* "Raiders Of The Lost Ark")

Remember this piece is a march! The music should be brisk, with a strong beat. Pay close attention to the dotted rhythms.

By John Williams

16
f
20
f
24
28
cresc.
D. 𝄋 (with repeat) al Coda
32
ff
mf
CODA
ff

Clair de Lune (from "Suite Bergamasque")

(*from* Ocean's Eleven)

This quiet, gentle piece was written originally for piano, and forms the third movement of the *Suite Bergamasque*. Since its composition in 1890, the music has been arranged for many different instrumental combinations.

By Claude Debussy

18
mp
21
24
27
30
cresc.
rit.
mf

Largo (from "Xerxes")
(*from* "Liaisons Dangereuse")

This famous piece began life as a song in the opera *Xerxes*, which was first performed in London in 1738. Largo means 'slow and broad'.

By George Frideric Handel